PauL

RASCAL THE DRAGON

Illustrated by Bob Lea

A RASCAL STORY

PUFFIN BOOKS

PUFFIN BOOKS

Published by the Penguin Group
Penguin Group (Australia)
250 Camberwell Road, Camberwell, Victoria 3124, Australia
(a division of Pearson Australia Group Pty Ltd)
Penguin Group (USA) Inc.
375 Hudson Street, New York, New York 10014, USA
Penguin Group (Canada)
90 Eglinton Avenue East, Suite 700,
Toronto, ON M4P 2Y3, Canada
(a division of Pearson Penguin Canada Inc.)
Penguin Books Ltd
80 Strand, London WC2R 0RL, England
Penguin Ireland
25 St Stephen's Green, Dublin 2, Ireland
(a division of Penguin Books Ltd)
Penguin Books India Pvt Ltd
11, Community Centre, Panchsheel Park, New Delhi-110 017, India
Penguin Group (NZ)
67 Apollo Drive, Rosedale, North Shore 0632, New Zealand
(a division of Pearson New Zealand Ltd)
Penguin Books (South Africa) (Pty) Ltd
24 Sturdee Avenue, Rosebank, Johannesburg 2196, South Africa

Penguin Books Ltd, Registered Offices:
80 Strand, London WC2R 0RL, England

First published by Penguin Books Australia,
a division of Pearson Australia Group Pty Ltd, 2004

13 15 17 19 18 16 14 12

Text copyright © Lockley Lodge Pty Ltd, 2004
Illustrations copyright © Bob Lea, 2004

The moral right of the author and illustrator has been asserted

Text design by Tony Palmer and Sandy Cull © Penguin Group (Australia)
Cover design by Sandy Cull © Penguin Group (Australia)
Illustration on inside front cover by
Andrew Weldon © Penguin Group (Australia)
Typeset in 14pt Stone Informal by Tony Palmer
Made and printed in China by Everbest Printing Co. Ltd
Colour reproduction by Splitting Image Colour Studio Pty Ltd,
Clayton, Victoria

National Library of Australia
Cataloguing-in-Publication data:

Jennings, Paul, 1943– .
Rascal the dragon.

ISBN 978 0 14 330036 6.

1. Dragons – Juvenile fiction. I. Lea, Bob, 1952– .
II. Title.

A823.3

puffin.com.au

Ben loved every dragon in the street.

'I wish Sniff was mine,' said Ben.
'Isn't he good?'

'No,' said Dad. 'He smells.'

'I wish Shovel was mine,' said Ben.
'Isn't he great?'

'No,' said Dad. 'He digs holes.'

'I wish Ruff-Ruff was mine,' said Ben.

'Isn't he terrific?'

'No,' said Dad. 'He barks.'

'I wish Bomber was mine,' said Ben.
'Isn't he fantastic?'

'No,' said Dad. 'He poos on people.'

'Can I have a dragon, please, Dad?'
said Ben. 'Just to love.'

'No way,' said Dad. He was cross
because he could not start the fire.

So Ben went out to play with Sniff.

And Shovel.

He played with Ruff-Ruff.

And Bomber.

Just then, Ben saw a small,
stray dragon.

'I wish you were mine,' said Ben.

'You are a little rascal.'

The stray dragon followed
Ben home.

'Maybe Dad will let me keep you,
Rascal,' said Ben.

'Dad, can I have this little
Rascal, please?' said Ben.
'No one wants him.'

'No,' said Dad. 'What good is he?
Can he wash the car?'

'No,' said Ben. 'But he is so nice.'

'Can he mow the lawn?' said Dad.

'No,' said Ben. 'But he is so lovely.'

'Can he hang out the washing?'
said Dad.

'No,' said Ben. 'But he is so cute.'

'Can he start the fire?' said Dad.

'Yes,' shouted Ben. 'He can.'

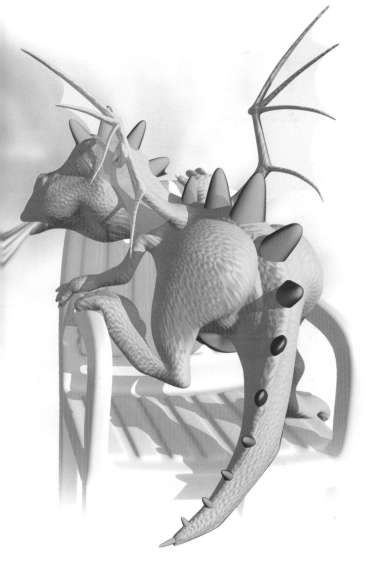

Dad was happy. 'You can keep
Rascal,' he said. 'He is amazing.'

'Yes, he is,' said Ben.
'And I love him.'